HUNDRED WORD HORROR
THE DEEP

Compiled & edited by A.R. Ward

To Kennedy,
Hold your breath!

Hundred Word Horror: The Deep

A Ghost Orchid Press Anthology

ISBN (paperback): 978-1-9196387-0-6

ISBN (e-book): 978-1-9196387-1-3

Cover design and book formatting by Claire Saag

Cover image © JM-MEDIA via Shutterstock

Interior Illustrations © GeoImages, GDJ, Vintage Illustrations and Yenty Jap via Canva.com

Full fathom five thy father lies;
Of his bones are coral made;
Those are pearls that were his eyes:
Nothing of him that doth fade,
But doth suffer a sea-change
Into something rich and strange.
Sea-nymphs hourly ring his knell:
Ding-dong.
Hark! now I hear them — Ding-dong, bell.

— *William Shakespeare*, "Full Fathom Five"
from *The Tempest*

CONTENTS

FOREWORD

Water: a source of both fascination and terror. A necessity for life, it inexorably draws us, even while we fear its dark, unyielding depths. What it gives, it can snatch away in the blink of an eye.

How calm the sea looks in the sunlight. How tempting. But what horrors lurk beneath that shining surface? Grasping tentacles? Alluring sirens? Killer riptides? We challenged our talented authors to explore the terrors of the ocean in only one hundred words. Just enough for you to dip your toe in. Perhaps you might even attempt to swim.

But please… try not to drown.

A.R. Ward

DEAD DRONES TELL NO TALES

1

Remember the Forgotten Beasts
by Dale Parnell

When men made

Of iron, oak and rope

Gather in low-lit rooms,

And haunted, haggard faces

Remember the sea,

Salted tears will tell tales

Of lost souls and demons

And of darkness undreamt of.

I beg of you, listen

And believe.

The stories there told,

Huddled around flickering flame,

Of ageless beasts that dwell in the deep

Serve as a warning to all

Who dare to brave an ocean squall.

For though we have forgotten those slumbering behemoths

They have not forgotten us,

They lie in wait

Ready to take back the seas,

And teach us our place

Once more.

DALE PARNELL lives in Staffordshire, England, with his wife and their imaginary dog, Moriarty. He writes fiction, mainly fantasy, science-fiction and horror, along with the occasional poem. He has self-published two collections of short stories and a poetry collection to date, and is featured in a number of excellent anthologies. You can find Dale on both Facebook and Instagram as @shortfictionauthor.

2

The Reservoir
by Katie Young

In the summer months, you can see the steeple of the drowned church, its cross rising up out of the reservoir like Excalibur.

But there are no legends about our village.

Our ruined homes lie forgotten in the dammed valley, the remnants of our past lives sitting quietly on the silt, beyond sunlight's reach.

Those who moved on were rewarded handsomely enough, but some of us would not be displaced. We huddled in the crypt as the water chased our breath out.

There are no tales of ghosts in the pipes, capsized boats, or missing children.

But there will be.

KATIE YOUNG is a writer of dark fiction. Her work appears in various anthologies including collections by Nyx Publishing and Fox Spirit Books, and her story, "Lavender Tea", was selected by Zoe Gilbert for inclusion in the Mechanic Institute Review's Summer Folk Festival 2019. She lives in North West London with her partner, an angry cat, and too many books. Her Twitter handle is @pinkwood.

3

Waiting for Death Alone
by Stephen Johnson

It has been four hours since I last saw anyone.

The storm clouds have passed and the sun has reached its apex as it bears down unmercifully on the surface of the now calm water. Debris covers the ocean as I clasp tightly to a chunk of wood that used to be the starboard bow.

The movement started about an hour ago.

Violent bumps pound my legs. The relentless sun shines down through the clear water allowing my nightmare to take a devilish form. I force myself to peer down below to see the crowded flurry of sharks circling underneath.

STEPHEN JOHNSON is a retired Naval Officer serving 22 years on four different ships over his career. He has published "The Hollow" in Eleanor Merry's Dark Halloween Holiday Flash Fiction Anthology *and "The Other Side of the Mirror" in Scare Street's* Night Terrors Volume 8.

.

4

Diver's Close Call
by K.M. Bennett

Foam slid off her as she tumbled onto the abandoned shore. She'd survived the encounter with that wild, grasping animal. Pink-touched rivers flowed from the fresh bite on her shoulder. Despite the wound, she was eager to get out into the water and do it again. She dumped the oxygen mask and tank in a hole with the others. The diver wouldn't be needing it anymore, after all. She swept a thick blanket of sand over the hole with her scaled tail. *It's only fair*, she thought. As long as the humans were destroying her home, there'd be no sightseeing.

K.M. BENNETT is a horror author living in the Midwestern U.S. with her husband, son, and spoiled Australian cattle dog. Her work has appeared on The NoSleep Podcast, The No Nap Podcast, and numerous small-press anthologies. More at ThatKatieLady.com or on Twitter at @That_Katie_Lady.

5

Dead Drones Tell No Tales
by Emma Kathryn

The Aboves had sent another robot. Its blinking eyes surveyed the great wreck she called home. Stalking carefully, she ensured it never caught her in its shuttered gaze. Once it got too close, she slammed her tail and smashed the camera. Talons tore it open, exposing its wired innards to the sea. Another drone dead.

Smiling, she dragged it through her ship. Through her ballroom, her theatre, her grand gallery. In the battered old engine room, she threw the corpse on a pile with eight others. Not one of them had seen her home and lived to tell the tale.

EMMA KATHRYN is a horror fanatic from Glasgow, Scotland. You can find her on Twitter @ girlofgotham. When she's not scaring herself to death, she is either podcasting as one half of The Yearbook Committee Podcast or she's streaming indie games on Twitch.

6

Trapped
by Yukari Kousaka

Translated by Toshiya Kamei

After a few weeks' deep ocean research, the penumbra descends upon us. The instruments on the control panel shriek. Our divers who went outside haven't returned. When I trace my index finger across the wall, a sticky substance smears on my fingertip. Liquid oozes from new cracks. I scramble away, heart pounding.

"This isn't an oil leak," our chief scientist cries as she raises her face from a microscope. "Stomach acid is eating through the ship!"

"The divers must've been digested!"

A drop hits my head and burns. The chief scientist gapes at the ceiling. I don't want to know.

Born in Osaka in 2001, YUKARI KOUSAKA is a Japanese poet, fiction writer, and essayist. Translated by Toshiya Kamei, Yukari's writings have appeared in The Crypt, New World Writing, *and* The Wondrous Real Magazine, *among others.*

7

Final Transmission of SSBN-873
by Cody Mower

S.O.S.
36°04'27 "N 159°26'00" W

Ballast Damaged. 15 dead. 17 injured. Damaged bulkhead sealed. Cannot get the vessel to rise. At approximately 02:45, encountered an unknown object at 235m. Sonar scan showed an 18m long anomaly moving 36m off starboard. Attempted radio contact, but the object was non-responsive. The thermal reading was inconclusive. Captain Muir thought it could be new Russian submarine technology until it swiped along the port side. It moved organically. Reactor and CO_2 scrubbers are still operational and are expected to remain active indefinitely. We are trapped.

S.O.S.
36°04'27 "N 159°26'00" W

CODY MOWER is a writer, veteran, and shaman based out of rural Maine, where he can be found casting runes, carrying boulders, or practicing ancient warfare tactics with a sword forged by a 9-fingered blacksmith. You can find his words in Moxy *and* Entropy Magazine, Love Letters to Poe, *Ghost Orchid Press,* The Dread Machine *and other spooky places. Follow Cody on Twitter @HeavyistheC.*

8

The Rise of Leviathan
by Adrian David

"Land ahoy!" Lieutenant Archibald adjusted his telescope, spotting a green dot amid the azure South Pacific Ocean. The Union Jack fluttered proudly on the mast of HMS Seeker.

The helmsman shuddered. "Many sailors speak fearfully about the mighty Leviathan lurking in these depths."

"Bollocks!" Archibald smirked. "That is—"

Grrr!

The expeditionary vessel lurched uncontrollably.

A gigantic serpentine creature rose from the abyssal waters, wrapping its mighty tentacles around the Seeker, capsizing it along with the dreams of the ambitious colonizers.

On an undiscovered island a nautical mile away, the Māori tribesmen concluded their ritual to Tangaroa, the Sea God.

ADRIAN DAVID writes ads by day and short stories by night. He dabbles in genres including horror, suspense, psychological drama, sci-fi, and everything in between, from the mundane to the sublime.

9

The Sirens of Sirenum
by Brianna Malotke

If you were a seasoned sailor

Then you knew all the rules

Of the sea.

And you would be sure

To have a supply of beeswax.

For if you came even just

A hair too close

To the Sirenum Scopuli islands

Then you took a risk

Of hearing the most charming

—absolutely bewitching—

Melodies carried by the wind.

And if you tempted fate

Your end would be theirs.

And as your ship sailed close

And you came upon them

—perched perfectly—

You would be clay in their hands

As they lounged within

A nest made from

Their still rotting victims.

BRIANNA MALOTKE is a freelance writer based in Illinois. You can find her work in the Hundred Word Horror anthologies, Beneath *and* Cosmos, *published in April and May of 2021. Looking ahead to 2022, she has two horror poems in the upcoming Women in Horror Poetry Showcase,* Under Her Skin, *published by Black Spot Books.*

10

Tunnel Vision
by Nikki R. Leigh

Pinned tight between the walls of the cave, I wait.

Wait for the air to run out or my mind to run out. Whichever comes first.

Sand kicks up around me—disturbed by what, I do not know. It clouds my vision; my eyes trapped behind goggles, trapped behind an ocean of pressure.

Limbs reach down to save me. No, not hands—snakes. Not snakes, not down here. Eels. They don't save. They bite.

My vision clouds again, red bleeding into the blue, mixing with the disturbed sand. A fresco of impending death.

The air gauge ticks down to 5%.

NIKKI R. LEIGH is a forever-90s-kid wallowing in all things horror. When not writing horror fiction, she can be found creating custom horror-inspired toys, making comics, and hunting vintage paperbacks. She reads her stories to her partner and her cat, one of whom gets scared very easily.
Instagram - @spinetinglers
Twitter - @fivexxfive
Email – spinetinglersmedia@gmail.com

11

Disposal
by Alice Mae Jameson

I like water. It's convenient. Powerful currents, especially, can remove detritus at a very satisfying pace. They're challenging, too. Some will drag your disposal package under in the space of a breath. Or not. Others will play with it, spinning it round, bouncing it up and down. Tantalising. That was the case with Jeffrey Durham. The current caught him right enough, bound in the smooth torpedo shape I'd chosen for him. But for one agonising moment he got caught in the wake of a passing boat. Just for a moment, and then he was gone. I like water. It's convenient.

ALICE MAE JAMESON lives in South West Scotland and is a writer of many things. She never stops trying and (so far) has never been stuck for ideas. She likes the bizarre and writes about the more gritty aspects of life.

12

Down in the Trenches:

Dr Montgomery's Observational Notes on Patient Jacob Carlson, Famed Oceanic Explorer

by T.L. Spezia

He screams when lights shut out or forced to shower.

Most disturbed patient I've ever treated.

Six months have transpired since recovery of one-man submarine, presumed lost. Still hasn't recounted explorations of Marianas Trench, nor explained bizarre scarification on hands and chest. Occasionally mutters, *"The lights! The lights!"*

Asked Jacob to draw (alternative to verbal communication).

Results: crude sketches of strange, webbed hands and glass orbs.

Says orbs "burned my mind!"

Says: "They made me look! I didn't want to! They made me look!"

Has said nothing of what *actually* happened. Holds to delusions.

More extreme treatments may become necessary.

T.L. SPEZIA writes short fiction and sometimes creative non-fiction in southeast Michigan. He edits Boneyard Soup, a horror & dark fantasy magazine. You can find him on Twitter at @timothyspezia.

.

13

Captain's Log
by Abi Marie Palmer

Day 3: That ship's mate I hired is nothing but a hindrance. Claimed he was an experienced seaman... Ha! My left boot would be more capable. Might let him go when we next make port (if not sooner).

Day 4: I caught the lad whistling today. Whistling! That's proof he's never sailed before. Everyone knows it's rotten luck to whistle at sea. Had the crewmen throw the fool overboard to appease the Atlantic Beast.

Day 5: The Beast attacked last night. Dragged six men to the depths. The wind whistled strangely afterwards... Almost cheerfully, as though it enjoyed our fate.

ABI MARIE PALMER is a writer and English teacher from the UK. You can find her fiction and poetry at abimariepalmer.com

14

Ariel Sails
by Clay F. Johnson

Nothing of him that doth fade,

But doth suffer a sea-change

Into something rich and strange.

Italian deeps the poet would not keep

And in no full fathom five did he lie,

No metamorphosed bones of sea-coral

And no pearly lustre glittered his eye—

Eyes that, when alive, glimpsed visions

Of gathering tempests, apparitions

In his own image, eidolons,

Doppelgängers Promethean

Dripping of sea-change transmutation:

Touched not by the worm-eaten grave

But with liquid fingers of soft decay,

Slipping from Ariel sails into unknown deeps,

Until, changed by rotting seas, he washed ashore

Recognized only by his book of Keats.

CLAY F. JOHNSON is an amateur pianist, devoted animal lover, and incorrigible reader of Gothic literature & Romantic-era poetry. His first collection of poetry, A Ride Through Faerie & Other Poems, *is forthcoming in 2021. Find out more on his website at www.clayfjohnson.com or follow him on Twitter @ClayFJohnson.*

15

Nicky the Swimmer
by Gus Wood

At the bridge,

Nicky the Swimmer tried to catch his breath.

This part got harder every time.

The snitch was wriggling, trying to escape and struggling against his

concrete shoes.

Nicky sighed and threw the guy over.

First the river bubbled, then it went still.

There was practically an army down there.

Nicky had lost count of the people he'd drowned.

That night, Nicky woke with a start.

The sheets were soaked.

In the dark, Nicky couldn't see.

He could only hear the scraping

of concrete getting closer

before the river filled his lungs.

First he bubbled. Then went still.

GUS WOOD is a game designer and horror writer. You can find his work at https://gusonhorror.com. He hopes you can read this underwater.

16

Endless Descent
by Alexis DuBon

They hang me at the gallows. The floor unhinges and opens beneath me. And I fall. I fall and I keep falling. The drop doesn't end.

Plummeting through air until I break through the waves, and I am sinking. Torpedoing through the darkest depths—deeper and deeper, my body shoots through water.

No yank on my neck, no *schwoop* of a rope snapping. Just an endless descent.

I've been submerged for longer than I can tell. We all breathe liquid in the womb. The body remembers.

And still, I plunge. I was promised a quick death, so many eons ago.

ALEXIS DUBON prefers morning to night and summer to winter, but she eats up dark and chilling stories like they're lasagna. You can find her in Home, Cosmos, *and* Beneath *from the* Hundred Word Horror *anthology series by Ghost Orchid Press, and on twitter @shakedubonbon.*

.

17

Intrepid Two
by Helen M. Merrick

The creature turns: its snake-like body, dotted with dazzling bioluminescence, twists like a demonic landing strip. Milky eyes cast around before fixing on my position. Its mouth opens, revealing a double row of razor-sharp teeth, as long as elephant tusks.

My searchlight bounces off something metallic stuck between the jagged fangs of the lower jaw. I gasp as I recognise part of Intrepid One's robotic claw.

Propellers slammed into reverse, I grip the joystick, praying forward momentum will cease. "Stop, please…" I whimper, willing the tiny submarine to respond.

Too late. The creature raises its monstrous head and lunges.

HELEN M. MERRICK lives in the UK Midlands with her family. When she's not teaching, she likes to scribble short stories and dream about writing a novel. She might, one day. You can find her at: www.authorhelenmerrick.wordpress.com

.

18

The Shipwreck of the Purgatory
by Ashley Hawk

Scattering fish dart through the buckled doors of the cruise ship, startled by the shark circling the wheelhouse.

Abandoned to the seabed, the shipwreck holds the echoes of panicked voices, clutching to the memories of those final screams.

Beams of sunlight filter down from the surface and dance across the rusting hull. They push through grimy windows, illuminating the endless halls with murky green light.

Spectres wander amongst the cabins, hovering over their own bloated bodies. These shadows—these forgotten souls, unaware of each other—they perish with the dying sun, and rise anew again at dawn.

Again.

Again.

Forever.

ASHLEY HAWK is a Creative Writing student in Cardiff, Wales, but started writing stories much younger at seven years old. Their stories often include LGBT+ characters and cover a whole range of genres. Whatever suits on the day. They are currently working on writing their first novel, a science-fiction YA Romance.

19

The Taste of Finding One Lost at Sea
by Cara Mast

I don't catch the fish anymore. Had to hire a man for that after the first few hundred eyes. Somewhere in there, I started seeing the sea. Not what was in front of me.

I was overjoyed. It was working.

My man puts more fish eyes in my hand. I don't count them, just shove the lot in my mouth. Savor the lenses' crunch, the slick gel. I swallow.

I'm ready.

I thank my man, dive off of his boat. On the tip of my tongue, the whole bay appears. Including you. I can finally sink back to your side.

As a retired tall-ship sailor, a failed academic, and a millennial finance professional, CARA MAST gets stopped constantly in New York City and asked for directions. Cara spends their free time drinking coffee, binging words, and yelling about the Philadelphia Eagles in their apartment and family group chat. They can be found on Twitter @digicara, and at digicara.com.

.

20

One of Many
by Sean Reardon

On the surface, she wore seduction. "If you love me, drink from me," she said. I didn't resist as she filled my lungs with water. The weight pulled me to her deepest caverns. When my feet reached the bottom, they merged with the silt and sand, solidifying at my shins. Three slices of skin flared open on either side of my neck, and I breathed in her infectious drink. I looked around. Thousands were melted to her ocean floor, all reaching upwards, towards that malevolent beauty. I reached for her, too. She teased in waves, and her laughter was deep.

SEAN REARDON is a burgeoning short story author with a penchant for the macabre. Follow him on Twitter (@batpocalypse) for more from his dark digest!

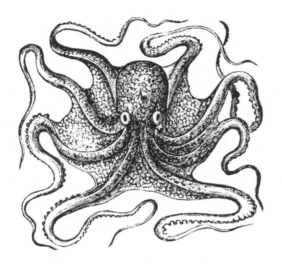

CATCH OF THE DAY

21

Fish Skin
by Vivian Kasley

I was born with it. Ichthyosis Vulgaris; fish scale disease. I'd daydream of flaying layers of my dry cracked flesh with a vegetable peeler until I was raw, bloody, and beautiful. Then one day I went to the beach, a place I'd always avoided. There was a quiet area in the sparkling emerald water near a cluster of slippery rocks. It's when I saw her. A human-like creature with skin like mine plucking a fiddler crab from the rocks and crunching it between her needle-sharp teeth. When she smiled and beckoned, I dove in to join her and never returned.

VIVIAN KASLEY hails from the land of the strange and unusual: Florida! She's a writer of short stories which have appeared in various science fiction anthologies, horror anthologies, horror magazines, and webzines. Her street cred includes Blood Bound Books, Dark Moon Digest, Gypsum Sound Tales, HellBound Books, Castrum Press, and Sirens Call Publications. She's got more in the works, including an upcoming tale in Vastarien *and her very first novella.*

You can find her on Facebook @bizzarebabewhowrites, Twitter @Vkasley and on Amazon: amazon.com/author/viviankasley.

22

Afternoon Snack
by E.C. Hanson

Her toes. So young. So perfect. They swayed back and forth in the murky water. Playful and carefree. Not realising. Not knowing. Not respecting the dangers below the boat. She wasn't raised to be afraid of the unknown. She wasn't raised to believe all of the recent rumours about sharks attacking children. She was raised to believe that life was a gift to be experienced with reckless abandon. Her dead parents taught her that. However, she wished she could reprimand her folks for that overrated advice. Because in a flash, she was inhaled by none other than a great white.

A graduate of NYU, E.C. HANSON's work has been published by Smith & Kraus and Applause Books in eight play anthologies. More than 35 of his plays have been developed and produced across the United States. His collection, All Things Deadly (Salem Stories), *will be released in August by D&T Publishing.*

23

Fish Food
by J.C. Robinson

Jack looked at his four red bellied piranha, swimming around in their tank. He loved them like people love their cats and dogs. They were his babies, loved. They hadn't eaten in five days, and they were looking gaunt.

Since losing his job, money had been tight, and he hadn't been able to afford their food. He needed to buy time till his unemployment kicked in, and he could afford the food again.

He knew what he had to do.

He walked over to the tank and lifted the lid. He stuck his arm into the water, and began to scream.

J.C. ROBINSON is a full-time law student, part-time writer. His debut novel, The Diner, *was published in March 2021. His works can be found in:* Hundred Word Horror: Beneath *and* Cosmos, *and* Hellhound Magazine Issue #1. *He is a member of the LGBT community, loves reading novels by Bentley Little, and has a cat he would gladly feed his arm to. Find him on twitter @jcr_scribe.*

24

Our Tradition
by Andrew McDonald

First day of fishing season is a day of celebration in my village. Villagers gather by the boats to sing songs and offer prayers of good fortune. It is our tradition.

The day before is not a happy one.

The sea can be cruel, so to ensure the safety of our fishermen and a bountiful harvest, tradition dictates an offering. This year I was chosen.

I am chained to a rock in the harbour. The elders speak the old words, everyone hides in their homes. When it comes for me, my cries will go unanswered. It is our tradition.

ANDREW McDONALD lives in St. John's, Newfoundland and Labrador, Canada with his wife and daughter. He is an avid listener of Heavy Metal, a proud collector of physical media and a reluctant fish owner.

25

The Depths of Your Stomach
by Toshiya Kamei

You pick me up between your fingers, throw your head backward, and open your mouth wide. Something hisses inside. There's no other choice. After a brief moment of hesitation, you pop me into your mouth and wash me down with Diet Coke. You gag briefly. I slide down your oesophagus, and your stomach acid burns my hazmat suit. I sink into the acrid depths of your stomach. I let myself float up, and my breath fogs up my gas mask. A stealthy creature snakes toward me, its red eyes flickering like twin fires. Unsheathing my katana, I hold it upward.

TOSHIYA KAMEI is a fiction writer whose short stories have appeared in New World Writing, Trembling With Fear, *and* Utopia Science Fiction, *among others.*

26

Catch of the Day
by Collin Yeoh

My child died in terror and agony. Suffocated. Butchered. Devoured.

Murdered.

You thought you got away with it. To dry land, where I could not touch you. Where I could only mourn, and rage, and gaze up at your impenetrable world. Helplessly. Impotently. For years and years. Till you thought your crime was forgotten.

And it was, wasn't it? *You* forgot it. You must have, because here you are in my domain again. In a craft as before, but larger. With more of your kind with you. Your family?

Well, then... watch them die now, just as my child did.

COLLIN YEOH spent 15 years writing advertising copy. He now spends his time writing things that have plots, characters, themes, genres, and that won't be subject to notes like "needs more product benefits." He lives in Bangkok and misses Malaysian food.

27

Cymothea
by James Dick

"Don't eat that fish," they said. They were right.

The snapper I'd caught at the pier had looked healthy. It had an undamaged body, clean scales, strong colour. Sure, it was a little small, but so what? It was still big enough for a meal. The only strange thing about it was that in place of a tongue there was a fat, yellow, beady-eyed bug.

I cut out the bug, cooked the fish, ate it. Now, standing in front of my bathroom mirror, I stared in horror at the two beady eyes twinkling at me from inside my own mouth.

JAMES DICK is an actor, author, screenwriter and director from Toronto, Ontario. His work has appeared or is upcoming in Improbable Press, Ghost Orchid Press, Dark Dragon Publishing, and Blank Spaces Magazine. *You can find him on Instagram at https://www.instagram.com/james.patrick.dick/.*

28

Widow's Walk
by Richard Martin

She stands on the balcony, hands gripping the railing as she leans forward, gazing out at the tranquil sea below. She'd come out here every day for how long now? Months? Years? Time had ceased to matter. It was habit, and deeply ingrained. She knew that, one day, he would come back for her.

He'd promised he would.

She closed her eyes, breathed deeply of the crisp sea air. Opening her eyes again, she took a reassuring glance down at the rifle leaning against the railings.

He had promised he would come back, and she would be ready for him.

RICHARD MARTIN started reading horror books at a young age, starting with R L Stine's Goosebumps *and* Point Horror *series'. He traumatised himself at the age of twelve when he read Stephen King's* IT *and never looked back. He is currently based in the UK, where he lives with his partner, and an inappropriate amount of books.*

29

The Waiting Game
by Blaise Langlois

As I dangle my feet in the cool of the water, I know I am tempting fate. This game I want to play needs a participant or two, and my sister, as usual, refused. Let her run off and tell mother then. Baby. The lagoon is dark and still. Some say, bottomless. Ridiculous. I know better. Finally, I see ripples across the water, radiating toward me like a beacon. With my lungs near bursting, I dive in head-first. Webbed fingers propel me forward. There's a flash of peach and red—lots of red. These teenagers are so easy to catch.

Emerging author, BLAISE LANGLOIS, will never turn down the chance to tell a creepy story. She has a penchant for horror, with published fiction and poetry through Eerie River Publishing, Pulp Factory E-zine, Black Spot Books, Ghost Orchid Press, Space and Time Magazine and Black Hare Press. Learn more at: www.ravenfictionca.wordpress.com.

30

Pond Life
by Jameson Grey

There's something in the pond at the end of the garden. I'm convinced of it. I keep catching glimpses of ripples in the water. As if something had surfaced, then quickly submerged again.

We only moved in last week. The previous owners made no mention of their keeping fish, although the pond seems a bit small for your typical pet koi. It looks deep though. Dark too. Probably needs a good clean.

Now, frankly, I'm worried. Our cat Fluffy was sniffing around there yesterday. He's gone missing. We found his collar floating on the pond surface. There were teeth marks.

JAMESON GREY is originally from England but now lives with his family in western Canada. He also spent time in Asia as a child, which he understands makes him a fully-fledged third culture kid (TCK). His fiction and poetry have been published by Ghost Orchid Press, Black Hare Press and Hellbound Books. He can be found online (occasionally) at jameson-grey.com and on Twitter @thejamesongrey.

31

Part of Your World
by Isaac Menuza

Water sloshes onto the grey beach from my truck bed. I rip the tarp off my industrial-sized tank. Junior scurries from it, tentacle legs smacking wet kisses on the glass.

His mother bobs in the surf, sings for him. That voice, man. Like an eel in my belly.

Junior dives under and is gone. Bye, son.

"He ate more than pizza and Skittles?" she asks. Purple tentacle breaks the surface, motions.

I place a cigarette in her lips, light it.

"God," she says, "I miss these most."

She takes a final drag, exhales a smile.

"See you in two weeks?"

ISAAC MENUZA is an author of speculative fiction and horror. He lives in Washington, D.C. with his wife, three children, and whatever slimy critters his son detains for temporary imprisonment. Find him on Twitter @Imenuza and at isaacmenuza.com.

32

Rescued?
by Emerian Rich

Standing over Jones, his breathing increasingly laborious, my resolve wavered. A dozen hungry mouths salivated nearby.

Zombies locked below deck called for his flesh. We pretended we weren't the same. The engines were dead, radio useless, and no...

"Land!"

Natives on shore cheered as we did. Coconuts high up in the trees brought tears to my eyes.

A boar roasted over a fire. Animal cages stacked nearby spoke of exotic tastes we'd willingly try. Out from a cage, a tiny paw reached out... or, no, tiny fingers clawed at the sand.

The look on the natives' faces was familiar. Hunger.

EMERIAN RICH is the author of the vampire series, Night's Knights. *She's been published in a handful of anthologies by publishers such as Dragon Moon Press, Hazardous Press, and White Wolf Press. Emerian is the horror hostess of the internationally acclaimed podcast, HorrorAddicts.net.*

33

Sushi
by Joe Haward

When the nuclear power station exploded fifty years ago, the sea surrounding it evaporated by half, tearing apart everything within its depths. Well, almost. A single creature survived; the humble jellyfish. But it was changed. Irrevocably. The research team, in full chemsuits, thought nothing existed there but scorched earth and poisoned water, the monstrous symphony of humanity's folly. Richard died first, pulled from the boat by impossibly large stinging tentacles. Ten days later the government nuked the sea, "as an act of containment." Seven weeks have passed, and we're the last stronghold as human sushi became nuclear nature's favourite dish.

JOE HAWARD is an eighth-generation oyster fisherman and Reverend with a love of the macabre. His second published book, Be Afraid, *explores the beauty and power of the horror genre in telling us about the world. He is also a freelance writer, husband, dad, and lover of cats. You can find him on Twitter @RevJoeHaward.*

34

The Price and the Prize
by Fliss Zakaszewska

Dark stone walls oozed moisture unpleasantly as water torrented down, but 'Indie' pushed them forward, gloomy mist chilling them to the marrow. The roar of the ocean thundered as they approached the end of the tunnel.

"Wait," cried his companion, stumbling, "it's getting deeper."

"We'll be OK," growled Jones, looking at the stonework. The ominous rumble made him stop, grip the other's hand, and haul him away as the dark bulk swept past.

"That was close. Damned street-cleaner's out late this evening." Jones looked across the road then down at his little boy. "There, son. McCoddy's; best fish-and-chips in Brigton-on-Sea.

Born in Guatemala to a British dad, FLISS ZAKASZEWSKA is living out lockdown by the sea in Cornwall. An MS365/SharePoint trainer by day and inveterate scribbler by night, Fliss' writing remit stretches from Technical Guides to flash fiction but her first novel is waiting for a discerning agent to snap it up. You can find her on Twitter @FlissZak.

35

Expunge
by Thomas E. Staples

All the infected shipmates were thrown into the watery abyss per the captain's orders.

Those with blotchy skin would rip human flesh from the bones of their fellow crew, and, with no cure on the ship, were tossed overboard for the safety of the others.

Three more hours before arrival—hauling a rare breed of splitfin fish back to England from the place no man should go—the captain culled his crew down to a meagre six.

Even long after they reached the safe shores, the captain hid the blotches of his own until he could conceal them no longer.

THOMAS E. STAPLES is a university graduate in Creative Writing and English Literature. With a love of both horror and comedy, they often smash the genres together very irresponsibly to see what happens. They have published multiple short stories since 2015 and published their debut novel, The Case of the Giant Carnivorous Worm, *in 2019.*
Twitter: @mrtestaples
Website: https://www.wrybrain.com/

36

Perfectly Built for Her Environment
by J.A. McCready

Even in this new body, I'm disorientated, my fall interrupted. AIDA transmits my thoughts through the crushing dark embrace of the deep sea up to the surface team.

Approx. 1000m. Hit a shelf. Mapping.

Roger.

Ragged layers of igneous rock. A sudden current whips up a blur of marine snow, drifting me towards a yawning cave where a yellow lantern glows. Inside, bioluminescent lights soar like tiny, welcoming campfires. Floating inside, my feet brush against a row of rocky spikes.

Like teeth. An anglerfish? *But—*

The cave snaps shut.

—I didn't know they could be so bi—

J.A. McCREADY lives in Ireland. A big fan of reading and writing all types of speculative fiction from high fantasy to horror, she can be found lurking on Twitter at @jenmcwriter.

37

Morning Swim
by Ian A. Bain

Dark waters reinvigorate tired skin
the bottom could be metres or kilometres away
swim, swim, swim   to the middle of the lake
completely alone.

It's hard to believe
no one else is on the lake
a perfect morning
for a swim.

Swim, swim, swim, seaweed tangle round ankles
try to kick it off, it holds, a tentacle
another wraps round the wrist, panic
sets in.

The weeds tighten their hold and pull down, face
barely above water, getting air in gasps
anotherweedgrabsthe
otherwristandanotherbindstheneckandthey'resqueezingandpulling
downand—

It's hard to believe

no one else is on the lake

a perfect morning

for a swim.

IAN A. BAIN (he/him) is a writer of dark fiction living in Muskoka, Ontario. Ian's work has recently appeared in Not Deer Magazine *and* The Crypt Online Magazine. *Ian can be stalked online at @bainwrites on Twitter.*

38

Plutonic Burgeoning
by Caity Scott

The whale songs blow through your body like wind through the stars, and your skin is stiff as wax. They can't be this deep, yet their dark shapes bow and rise on the radar, weaving your way.

The cries rumble louder, shivering your ship. Though encased in metal, you are exposed. Shell-less. And as soon as it starts, the melody curves flat. It's not silence—not the lack of sound—but sound devoured and turned in on itself.

Blackness fizzles, pricks the walls, the lights, the air. As coldness splinters, your skin bubbles and bursts. Your jaw dissolves before you can scream.

CAITY SCOTT writes about diabolical joy, simple wonder and (whenever possible) dinosaurs. When she's not listening to murder podcasts, she's pursuing an MFA in creative writing at Western Washington University. Her work can be found in Jeopardy Magazine *and* The Disappointed Housewife.

39

Spirit Pool
by Elizabeth Eckstein

Don't swim in the spirit pool, they said. It's cursed, they said. Nonsense, Tamsyn thought.

The silky black water caressed her ankles, then her calves as she stepped in. Her reflection shimmered moonlit bright, returning her plucky smile. A flurry of wind, quick as a breath, ruffled her hair and brushed her cheek.

Nothing to be afraid of.

She pushed down on her dress as it ballooned around her, her cocky reflection smiling wide. Wider. A hungry snarl set on its face as Tamsyn slipped under, choking, sinking. Her eyes stared wildly as her watery doppelganger rose from the surface.

ELIZABETH ECKSTEIN is a storyteller and lover of thunderstorms, a coffee-soaked alchemist who lives amongst the pages of books. When not creating worlds with words, she brings them to life in digital art as book illustrations and covers. A devourer of classics and folder of origami birds, she is the creator of The Crucible of the Crimson Lion *series. You can find her on Twitter @RedElixier, Amazon: https://www.amazon.com/~/e/B089G6PQ32 or on Instagram @thecrucibleofthecrimsonlion.*

40

Bath Time
by Dale Parnell

"Is he still in the bath?" Dad asked.

"You know he loves it," Mum replied nervously.

"Dad, look; shark!" Callum grinned.

"He's too old for bath toys," Dad yelled, snatching it from his son's hand.

Later that night, Callum heard Dad's drunken raging, and Mum's injured tears.

On Sunday evening, as his father took a bath, Callum found the toy shark, and dropped it into the bath water.

"Why you little…" was all Dad could manage, now suddenly alone in a vast, freezing ocean, as a twelve-foot Great White circled close by.

"Shark," whispered Callum, staring into the empty bathtub.

DALE PARNELL lives in Staffordshire, England, with his wife and their imaginary dog, Moriarty. He writes fiction, mainly fantasy, science-fiction and horror, along with the occasional poem. He has self-published two collections of short stories and a poetry collection to date, and is featured in a number of excellent anthologies. You can find Dale on both Facebook and Instagram as @shortfictionauthor.

THALASSOPHOBIA

41

The Locker
by Eric Fomley

Water surrounds my body, crushing me. Everything sounds distorted. I try to scream.

~~~

It's warm. I'm standing in front of a scarred and ancient door. A man sits on a high-backed chair beside it. A konch grows from the side of his eyeless face. The legs of a sand crab protrude from between his eyelids.

"Where am I?" I ask him. I'd just been on the boat with my dad but then... what?

The black holes in his face seem to look up at me, like he knows what I'm thinking. He gives me a sad smile.

"You never left."

ERIC FOMLEY is a member of SFWA. His stories have appeared in Daily Science Fiction, Flame Tree, *and* The Black Library. *You can follow him and his work on Twitter @PrinceGrimdark or on his website ericfomley.com.*

42

Solution
by Philine Schiller

The bubbles disintegrate gently as you sink into the warm water of your bathtub. Smiling, you dive under and open your eyes. Blurry light flickers above you. You reach out your hand, expecting it to touch air, but it doesn't. You reach further, confused. Still nothing. You try to sit up, but you keep slipping, sinking, trying not to panic, not to breathe. The lights diminish. Desperate, your hands reach for the plug. It comes loose suddenly, like your mouth. The water gurgles, and there's nothing left in the bathtub when the last drops of you glide down the drain.

PHILINE SCHILLER is a doctoral student at the University of Heidelberg, Germany, where she received her M. Ed. for English and Spanish philology and currently works as research assistant. Her academic and literary interests include contemporary literature, food studies, popular culture, fantasy, horror and science-fiction.

43

Octopoda
by Caitlin Marceau

The cold does little to distract him from the blistering pain inside his chest.

He'd always hated octopi. Their freakish limbs and soft bodies repulsed him, unless they were battered and fried. The only way he liked them, he'd joke, was dead.

Their feelings for him were mutual.

He convulses as one of the creatures forces their way down his throat and into his body, the others pining him to the ocean floor. He gags, broken jaw limp and stretched wide, slowly drowning, as one arm reaches deep into his belly.

He'd devoured their brethren.

The octopi wanted them back.

CAITLIN MARCEAU is an author and lecturer living and working in Montreal. She holds a B.A. in Creative Writing, is a member of both the Horror Writers Association and the Quebec Writers' Federation, and spends most of her time writing horror and experimental fiction. She's been published for journalism, poetry, as well as creative non-fiction, and has spoken about horror literature at several Canadian conventions. Her collections, A Blackness Absolute *and* Palimpsest, *are slated for publication by D&T Publishing LLC and Ghost Orchid Press in 2022 respectively. If she's not covered in ink or wading through stacks of paper, you can find her ranting about issues in pop culture or nerding out over a good book. For more, check out CaitlinMarceau.ca.*

44

Sea Witch
by Waverly X Night

It was early autumn when the terror took our town. Women, young and old, healers and harlots, were dragged from their homes and thrown into the churning sea to prove their innocence.

I had never had power, but I had a stubbornness that vexed the men endlessly. They tossed me into the water, hoping to finally be rid of me.

When I rose again, drowned but not dead, they threatened me with shackles and said to kneel. How silly of them to think that I would prostrate myself if I survived.

They called me a witch, so I became one.

WAVERLY X NIGHT is a writer, an engineer, and an avid believer of magic. When she isn't writing, she likes practicing aerial hoop in preparation for the day she inevitably runs away to join the circus. Find her on Instagram @livesbetweenwords or at www.waverlyxnight.com.

45

Reunion
by Yuki Fuwa

Translated by Toshiya Kamei

Our ship submerges deeper and deeper, and in my mind's eye, my daughter trails a tiny finger down the map of the ocean in my study.

"Nobody has reached the depths we have."

I bark the order for my crew to start our assent. I grab the comm and talk to my wife on the surface. "Honey, a celebration is in order." She's been distant since our daughter's death.

"Sir, the weights refuse to budge."

"What?"

"Daddy, I've missed you!" A girl's voice echoes through the ship. "We're together again." It's my daughter. My wife's laughter crackles through the comm.

YUKI FUWA is a Japanese writer from Osaka. In 2020, she was named a finalist for the first Reiwa Novel Prize. In the same year, her short story was a finalist in the first Kaguya SF Contest. Translated by Toshiya Kamei, Yuki's short fiction has appeared in Litro *and* New World Writing.

46

Undersea
by Belicia Rhea

Inside her shell is the tide is the waves is your tomb. You remember iridescence, a song, kelp in your mouth. Salt in your lungs. It burns when your sides split open to inhale bloody water through your wounds. A blur. She's kissing you, her tongue an eel sliding slow over your tongue and you're writhing, your breath fills like a well. Your slick legs fuse and her sparkling tail is wrapped around you, dragging you down in the deep, and finally, you breathe. Black water sways above, below, and inside of you—the glimmer of the shore long gone.

BELICIA RHEA was born under a waning crescent moon in the Sonoran Desert. Her work spans genres, often leaning dark. She writes short and long form, prose and poetry, and the spaces in-between.

47

Grasping
by C.J. Dotson

When people notice how I hate water, how I can't so much as look at anything bigger than the puddle that collects at the bottom of my driveway after storms—and, god, even that's bad, isn't it?—they nod, say things like "aquaphobia".

Maybe they're right. On a family vacation, in a distant place and a distant time, I watched my sister drown.

Nobody notices how I hate hands, how I can't look at them. When I refuse a handshake, they ask if I have OCD. That's when they're wrong.

I saw the long, slick fingers... They dragged her down.

C.J. DOTSON lives with her large family in a creepy old house in the American Midwest, where she writes horror, sci fi, and fantasy flash, short stories, and novels. In her spare time she enjoys painting and baking. For more stories, check out cjdotsonauthor.com. Visit her as @cj_dots on Twitter.

48

Heavier Than Oceans and Seas
by Marisca Pichette

He handed it to me, rim encrusted with salt.

"Drink," he said. "Drink, and you'll never sink."

His face drifted before me, tentacles splayed.

I thought about dropping it. Spilling the brine between us to disperse into the shadows of the cave. Swimming away from here; from him. Letting the currents displace my tears.

A tentacle encircled my wrist. My fingers went cold as the cup neared my lips.

"Drink."

Sharper than the sea, brine stung. I swallowed, expecting salt—tasting blood. I dropped the cup then, convulsing as I dried from the inside out.

He was right.

I float.

MARISCA PICHETTE is a bisexual author of speculative fiction, nonfiction and poetry, living in Western Massachusetts. Her work has been published in PseudoPod, Daily Science Fiction, Apparition Lit, *and* The NoSleep Podcast, *among others. She is on Twitter as* @MariscaPichette.

49

Monstruo
by Anastasia Garcia

The jungle drums are deafening, like blood pounding through my veins.

A cloak of coloured feathers weighs heavy on my shoulders, as do the necklaces of jade and gold. I walk barefoot towards the wide-mouthed *cenote* where the water glows an ethereal blue, beckoning for a fresh sacrifice.

Beneath the shining surface the *monstruo* awakes, unfurling in a writhing mass of black scales, slip-slithering in the depths like a great snake.

I march on, for I am chosen. If the beast consumes me, then I was never fit to rule. But if I survive… then I will be Queen.

ANASTASIA GARCIA is a Mexican-American writer of horror and speculative fiction. Anastasia's writing is featured in the Lunatics Radio Hour Podcast, Corvid Queen, and the Nottingham Horror Collective. Originally from Texas, Anastasia now lives in New York City with her partner and her cats. Follow her writing journey on Instagram @anastasiawrites or at anastasiawrites.com.

50

Tell Tail Siren
by Maria Ann Green

It was my song that killed her.

Human taking siren.

My innocently grinning lips. Liars.

Her fate sealed with one look. Her tail, her hair, rainbows reflecting back my hungry expressions. Her nipples jeweled with scales tasted like strawberries and seawater as they slid down my throat.

But months later, even dead, she keeps screaming inside my head. Trying to swim out. Every time I open my mouth, her voice hides inside my words. Slowly becoming more her words too, her thoughts.

Glug, glug.

Sounds, not words, come from my blue lips now. Lips tasting more like hers every day.

MARIA ANN GREEN is a USA Today and internationally bestselling indie author of horror, thrillers, and romance. She's also had short fiction published in literary journals such as Prologue *and* Read This Damnit! *She's a proud bisexual and a warrior of both chronic pain and anxiety. Above all, she believes every story has a reader. You can find all of her links at: linktr.ee/mariainmadness*

51

Sirens
by Caytlyn Brooke

The villagers roared, drunk on fervour. They bound the young women with coarse ropes, weighed their ankles with heavy stones.

"Drown the witches! Send them back to Hell!" they screamed.

The three women pleaded their innocence, but their cries fell on deaf ears. All at once, the mob pushed them off the jagged cliffs, cheering as their bodies plummeted beneath choppy black waves. As salt water filled their lungs, the Devil appeared. He saved their souls, gifting them beautiful voices in exchange for their servitude.

Now, the women haunt the shores, weaving hypnotic lullabies, calling their murderers to watery graves.

CAYTLYN BROOKE is an award-winning author who enjoys creating horror stories from mundane rituals of daily life. With a degree in psychology, she studied fears and stimuli that make people uncomfortable. When she's not writing, she runs a daycare. She promises there are no children buried in the backyard. You can find her on Twitter @caytlyn_brooke or at:
https://www.bhcpress.com/Author_Caytlyn_Brooke.html

52

The Shelf
by wren andrea

we thought we'd gone

as deep as we could, three moons past,

like comets like wishes like scales

flying over that surface

we find even more terrifying

than what this edge, this line we touch

with our tentacles, holds.

we look over the edge, you and i

into void, hear

echoes from that ink blank below

urging us, propelling us, sirening

the water's fine

though we know those voices—

we've searched

the floor of the earth for them.

we wrap

our suckers around and around until

we slide off, tethered not to the floor beneath

but only to each other.

WREN ANDREA (she/they) is a writer and recent graduate of the Stonecoast MFA Program. They write science fiction, horror stories, and poetry—her most recent project being a novel written from the perspective of an octopus. Their words can be found in the Stonecoast Review, Waves to Sea, *and on Twitter @wren_is_sleepy*

53

Orphaned by Birth
by Micah Castle

Upon the shore, it lies. Translucent, thinly flayed flesh blooming from its middle, revealing grey-purple folds of soft membrane holding at bay now-lifeless viscera. The murky tide waxes over its discharged womb, the long unfurling tails spilling into the fathomless sea.

Curling fog occults the bleak horizon, shielding us from light. Men will arrive soon, carrying rusted tools and blazing torches. Even now, I hear their belligerent screams.

I know I have to leave; have to preserve in this cold, damp world. Like the umbilical cord that once tethered us, our connection must be severed and we must part.

MICAH CASTLE is a weird fiction and horror writer. His stories have appeared in various places, and he has three collections currently out. He enjoys spending time with his wife, aimlessly hiking through the woods, playing with his animals, and can be found reading a book somewhere in his Pennsylvania home. You can find him on Twitter @micah_castle, Reddit r/MicahCastle, and on micahcastle.com.

54

Thalassophobia
by C. A. Chesse

My husband came back from his vacation as video footage from his scuba helmet.

Something went wrong on his dive: he was caught in a current and sucked into an undersea canyon. He looks up, watching the light disappear; looks down, at darkness like a vast, open mouth.

Then he flails and screams.

Inside me, our daughter hears his voice and flails too, panicked into birth. It is too late for him, too soon for her. Both are drowning.

I always feared sharks. But now I know; there need be nothing in the water. The monster is the deep itself.

While she was pregnant with her first child, C. A. CHESSE happened across a documentary about a diver who was sucked off an undersea cliff, where he died in extreme pressure, cold and total darkness. She has had mild thalassophobia ever since. She can be reached at @CAChesse on Twitter.

55

Bloom
by Steve Neal

The Agatha washed ashore unmanned, four weeks after its last broadcast: an SOS, speaking of an alga clogging up the motors, leaving them adrift.

A purple substance coated the interior of the small fishing vessel from ceiling to floor. A viscous, bulbous tissue that looked like bruised muscle fibers stretched and layered atop one another. It expanded and deflated at random, fist-sized spots ballooning up as if taking a deep breath.

An oddly shaped lump in the corner was lighter than the rest, seemingly a newer formation. It twitched and managed to croak out two final, wheezed words. "Burn it."

STEVE NEAL is an English-born writer currently surviving the summers of Florida with his supportive wife and less supportive cats. As a lifelong horror fanatic, he enjoys poking at the unknown and seeing what comes crawling out, as long as it isn't spiders.

56

Night Diver
by Katie Young

You can only fully appreciate the colours of marine life by night, when the pure white light from your torch reveals the true extent of its bright beauty. I've been diving for years, and the reef takes my breath away every time.

My beam sweeps over the shifting hues of coral, fish, and crabs on the ocean bed scuttling for the cover of darkness. It briefly illuminates an octopus jetting into the inky black beyond. I turn three-hundred-and-sixty degrees, the torchlight just catching a flash of something pale and humanoid seconds before I feel a hand fasten around my ankle…

KATIE YOUNG is a writer of dark fiction. Her work appears in various anthologies including collections by Nyx Publishing and Fox Spirit Books, and her story, "Lavender Tea", was selected by Zoe Gilbert for inclusion in the Mechanic Institute Review's Summer Folk Festival 2019. She lives in North West London with her partner, an angry cat, and too many books. Her Twitter handle is @pinkwood.

57

Albatross
by T.L. Spezia

Albatross carry the souls of dead sailors, so I should have plenty to eat when one lands on the portside railing. Our ship ran aground after a storm. Mast destroyed; provisions gone.

I snatch the bird. My knife makes easy work of its belly. Raw gore slips out, along with half-chewed fingers and an eyeball. The grizzly sight of these nautical souls is nauseating.

The deck is littered with the violated bodies of my crewmates. Those still alive are sustained by the carrion flesh.

A shriek above: Hundreds of albatross fill the sky, circling the scraps of this taboo feast.

T.L. SPEZIA writes short fiction and sometimes creative non-fiction in southeast Michigan. He edits Boneyard Soup, a horror & dark fantasy magazine. You can find him on Twitter at @timothyspezia.

58

Ad Meliora
by Hazel Ragaire

The best belong to me: Loch Ness, Kraken, Leviathan, Lyngbakr. Rising from the deep, antiquity's monsters destroyed and bore harpoon and gunpowder scars with pride. My modern monsters know size doesn't determine devastation. And so they recalibrated themselves: sulfur-based life flourishes now, disdaining the sun. It gathers, basking in the vents, pulsing, changing, waiting for evolution's inevitability. A watery world is all they desire, and they will slip inside, acclimating to a body made of 60% water, offering 140 grams of sulfur: a buffet. They will trade my depths for a new frontier made of flesh and blood and bone.

Only ideas outnumber the horror books residing in HAZEL RAGAIRE's home. After years of teaching, Hazel decided to breathe life into words. When she's not conjuring up new characters or worlds, you'll likely find her plotting. Her favorite word is airneán, and you're welcome to join her anytime. Find her on Facebook to find published works or works in progress.

59

...And the Muckers Came Out
by Isaac Menuza

The town drank the lake dry, and the muckers came out.

First one to go was little Heidi. They found her in the cratered lake bed, torso buried in the mud, pinstriped leggings jutted like TV antennas. She'd only wanted a drink.

At night, townspeople woke to hear the wet suction of the muckers' steps on the street, the screams of their victims. Morning sun dried trails of brown and red sludge through broken windows.

Before long, the town moved, next lake over. Current residents resisted. They screamed, too.

The survivors drank the lake dry, and the muckers came out.

ISAAC MENUZA is an author of speculative fiction and horror. He lives in Washington, D.C. with his wife, three children, and whatever slimy critters his son detains for temporary imprisonment. Find him on Twitter @Imenuza and at isaacmenuza.com.

60

The Wall
by Brooke Percy

As Elle reclined on the beach, eyes closed, she felt the warmth of the sun disappear. She opened her eyes—expected to see a cloud bank, but found an approaching wall of water. The tidal wave bore down on her as she watched, helpless. It hit with unimaginable force.

Elle was swept up in the cold, roiling mass of water; swirled as her brain struggled to adjust to the sudden change in situation. Her unprepared lungs strained for breath; her limbs flailed in an effort to gain control, to find the surface. Instead, Elle only found more water.

Then, darkness.

BROOKE PERCY is a lifelong, voracious writer and reader of stories. She lives in Ontario, Canada with her family and two dogs, who are excellent sounding boards for her writing. Brooke posts daily Microfiction on Twitter at: https://twitter.com/BrookePercy1, and is excited to share her writing through other mediums as well.

UNLUCKY DIP

61

Fully Submerged
by Brianna Malotke

He closed his eyes,

As he stood along the ocean's edge,

With the salty breeze

Wafting through his memories.

Images of fair maidens swimming,

Their long hair loose, floating around them—

With songs like sirens, skin rough—

Their arms outstretched, gesturing

For him to join them deeper.

Longing to join them, he willingly went

Into the icy sea,

Until fully submerged under,

The salt stinging his eyes and filling his lungs.

Soon they surrounded him, hands caressing,

The last image he saw was their smiles,

Spreading wide—as fear spread through him—

Exposing sharp white teeth,

Eager to devour him.

BRIANNA MALOTKE is a freelance writer based in Illinois. You can find her work in the Hundred Word Horror anthologies, Beneath *and* Cosmos, *published in April and May of 2021. Looking ahead to 2022, she has two horror poems in the upcoming Women in Horror Poetry Showcase,* Under Her Skin, *published by Black Spot Books.*

62

Whale Song
by Gus Wood

After ten years, the Translator works.

Time to field-test it.

Fourteen months training. Two more on the submarine.

Once we're deep enough,

I use the radar to boost my Translator's signal.

No contact.

Then we find them.

"Black Whales."

Only rumours until now.

All big as starships and filling the depths with their strange song.

My device flickers as it translates:

"At last," it says.

No time to ponder the words

Before the radar sounds again.

"Oh God," one of the technicians says.

"We can eat."

The Translator's voice is the last sound I hear before teeth pierce the hull.

GUS WOOD is a game designer and horror writer. You can find his work at https://gusonhorror.com. He hopes you can read this underwater.

63

Organism
by K. J. Watson

Nilsen's belief in a legendary, thalassic organism damaged his career as a marine biologist. But when a harmful algal bloom approached the coast, he saw an opportunity for redemption.

Attaching a fine-mesh net to a boat, he towed the bloom to an isolated fjord. Here, the algae rotted and consumed the water's oxygen.

The subsequent aquatic disruption caused a suffocating, primordial beast to surface.

"The Kraken!" Nilsen shouted. "It exists!"

Foolishly, though, he'd failed to consider what might happen next. The monster surged from the fjord and disappeared out to sea. As did Nilsen, clutched between the fabled organism's jaws.

K. J. WATSON's fiction has appeared on the radio; in magazines, comics and anthologies; and online. His website is at https://k-j-watson.webnode.co.uk.

64

Beyond the Sea
by Marc Sorondo

I didn't think.

I'd missed him so badly and for so long, when I saw my dad standing out there, waving, beckoning me, I just started swimming.

I swam until my lungs felt like they would burst and my shoulders ached. As I got close and glanced up, I saw the roots—like trails of leafless kelp—trailing down from where his feet should have been and into the black deep.

By then I was too close. It was too late to think, too late to swim away.

He embraced me and, together, we sank down into the crushing abyss.

MARC SORONDO lives with his wife and children in New York. He loves to read, and his interests range from fiction to comic books, physics to history, oceanography to cryptozoology, and just about everything in between. He's a perpetual student and occasional teacher. For more information, go to MarcSorondo.com.

65

The Princess and the Sea Witch
by Anastasia Garcia

The sea witch is near.

I call her with a drop of blood in the water, as I did the first time many years ago.

My lover languishes in the sun, unaware. His muscles ripple with a sweat-slicked sheen. "Mi princesa has beauty, brains, wealth, and power. How am I so lucky?" he asks, with a bright, boyish grin.

I think of the sea witch picking her teeth with his glistening white bones. "I made a deal."

"A deal? With whom?" He asks.

The sea witch breaks the water's surface with a face split by too many teeth.

He screams.

ANASTASIA GARCIA is a Mexican-American writer of horror and speculative fiction. Anastasia's writing is featured in the Lunatics Radio Hour Podcast, Corvid Queen, and the Nottingham Horror Collective. Originally from Texas, Anastasia now lives in New York City with her partner and her cats. Follow her writing journey on Instagram @anastasiawrites or at anastasiawrites.com.

66

The Water That Licks
by Josh Sippie

At first it tickles, almost teasingly. Like loose bristles of a never-used linen paintbrush, running along the bottom of my feet. From my dead man's float, I sit up, sink a little. The same soft bristles sneak up behind, running the length of my spine. I spin to confront it, but it's gone again and I sink more, unable to find the calm to float again. I look down into the water beneath me and see the shadow, lurking underneath. Small at first—the size of a grapefruit—but enlarging quickly until it opens, pushing the swell up over me.

JOSH SIPPIE lives in New York City, where he's the Director of Publishing Guidance at Gotham Writers and an Associate Editor at Uncharted Mag. *His writing can be found at* McSweeney's Internet Tendency, The Writer Magazine, Sledgehammer Lit, Wretched Creations, Hobart, Not Deer, *and more. More at joshsippie.com or @sippenator101.*

67

One Little Push
by Collin Yeoh

Just one little push.

It'd be so easy, wouldn't it? Here out in the open sea, with no land in sight. We're cruising so fast, we'll leave her far behind in minutes. And this railing really is dangerously low.

One little push when no one's watching...

...and all of Dad's millions will be mine alone.

God, what am I thinking? I'm no murderer! Sure, we can't stand each other and never have, but she's still my sister! This is insane!

Maybe it's time we reconciled. Once Dad's gone, we'll be the only family we have left. I'll try to taa*aiiieee*

COLLIN YEOH spent 15 years writing advertising copy. He now spends his time writing things that have plots, characters, themes, genres, and that won't be subject to notes like "needs more product benefits." He lives in Bangkok and misses Malaysian food.

68

Deep in the Pit of His Stomach
by Patrick Barb

Down inside the patient's stomach, with no hope of extraction or reversal of the shrinking process, the doctor watches from her submersible as digestive juices recede. The path from esophagus and out of the mouth is no longer viable.

No word from the "surface" since the last message: someone crying out, "Everyone's dying up here."

Designed for temporary surgical extraction, the craft's shielding won't hold much longer against the desperate enzymes' attacks. Light works differently at this miniature size. She's starting to mistake his stomach tumor for a god.

It pulses, feeding on fetid water. She feels compelled to worship.

PATRICK BARB is a freelance writer and editor from the southern United States, currently living (and trying not to freeze to death) in Saint Paul, Minnesota. Previously, his short fiction has appeared in Sci-Fi & Scary, *Crystal Lake Publishing's* Shallow Waters Vol. 7, Boneyard Soup Magazine, *and other publications. For more of his work, visit patrickbarb.com and follow him at twitter.com/pbarb.*

69

Lake Tours
by Dale Parnell

The tour boat chugged across the iron-flat water, falling silent as the Skipper killed the engine.

"Lake Brendan is the third deepest lake in the world," the tour guide continued, her voice crackling over the loudspeakers. "And the legend of its famous monster has been around for hundreds of years."

As if on cue, something large and heavy struck the hull, eliciting a few panicked screams.

"He's impatient today," the Skipper whispered, sidling up beside the tour guide.

"It's been a few weeks," she replied. "He's hungry."

"Okay then, folks," the Skipper called, merrily. "Who's first in the diving cage?"

DALE PARNELL lives in Staffordshire, England, with his wife and their imaginary dog, Moriarty. He writes fiction, mainly fantasy, science-fiction and horror, along with the occasional poem. He has self-published two collections of short stories and a poetry collection to date, and is featured in a number of excellent anthologies. You can find Dale on both Facebook and Instagram as @shortfictionauthor.

70

Siren in the Shower Drain
by Brandon Applegate

Another dollop of his flesh thumps to the floor of the shower, spins in the pink current, slithers down the open drain.

Her song floats up from the pipes, numbs him, tells him he must go to her.

He carves off a length of forearm. The hank plops to the tile, slips into the hole, another piece of him that will join her in the sea.

Vision blurs. *Blood loss*. In black flashes he sees her, naked, smooth curves floating in the blue. She slides a piece of him between her needle-like teeth. This is how they will be together.

BRANDON APPLEGATE writes weird and dark fiction near Austin, TX. He moonlights at a local tech company, and spends his weekends with his wife and two girls. You can find him on Twitter @brandonappleg8 or at bapplegate.com.

71

Millions of Microscopic Eggs
by Russell Nichols

Your tongue is going numb.

Over sirens your wife says: "He swallowed too much water!"

The paramedic pushes you on the gurney. "Did you not see the 'Water Hazard' sign?"

Your wife wanted to row there.

"He wanted to row there," she says.

"That 'water' was Incubarb fluid containing millions of microscopic eggs."

Your wife told you about this sea creature—just before capsizing your kayak.

"It was what?!"

"We must sever the tongue, but I need your permission—"

"My permission? I can't—"

"Your husband cannot speak. Please. Time is of the essence."

"It's his choice!"

Your whole mouth is burning.

RUSSELL NICHOLS is a speculative fiction writer and endangered journalist. Raised in Richmond, California, he got rid of all his stuff in 2011 to live out of a backpack with his wife, vagabonding around the world ever since. Look for him at russellnichols.com.

72

The Woman in the Lake
by Nico Bell

The bottom of the lake was no place for a lady. Olivia frowned as her bloated ankle once again got caught in the kelp.

A splash disrupted the lake's surface. A spark of hope ignited in Olivia as she swam up and spotted a woman treading water.

Jealousy soured Olivia's dry mouth. She moved quickly, grabbed the startled woman's shoulders, and kissed her. The woman barely had a chance to scream before her life surged through Olivia's body, awakening long lost parts. She released the woman, now pale and wide-eyed, and watched her sink.

Olivia smiled and swam to shore.

NICO BELL is the author of horror novella Food Fright *and the editor of horror anthology* Shiver. *She's had several short stories published in both horror and romance. She can be found at www.nicobellfiction.com and on Twitter and Instagram @nicobellfiction.*

73

Look Who's Here
by Renata Pavrey

Peering over a lake, she watches the face rippling in front of her. If only it knew what lay beyond its glassy surface. She smiles at the water, but is met with angry eyes and a scowling face. "I thought you always parted your hair to the right. New look?" asks Hannah, wondering why her friend's nose ring has also switched to the other side. The reflection turns away from the lake and walks towards Hannah. Maya pounds from below the watery grave, calling out to her friend to be rescued from the depths of what has taken her place.

RENATA PAVREY is a nutritionist by profession, specializing in clinical and sports nutrition. She is a Pilates teacher, a trained Odissi dancer, a marathon runner, and bibliophile. Her writings cover a broad spectrum of subjects including dance, literature, running and other sports, health and fitness, nature and wildlife, languages, movies, and music. You can find her @tomes_and_tales and @pilates_positivity_with_ren on Instagram, at https://medium.com/@reneemarianne7 on Medium, and on her blog www.tomesandtales365.wordpress.com.

74

Siren
by Ashley Hawk

Down here, talons of sunlight pierce through the gaps in the rocks and turn the roiling water green. These caves—the sharp rocks, the frigid currents—they beckon him.

It's silent, still. Except—

The song drifts out from a crevasse hidden deep within the cavern's maw. It corrodes his thoughts, echoing the lullaby his husband sang their son last night.

Entranced, he floats over the ocean floor, the beam of his torch sweeping over scattered bones wrapped in ribboned flesh.

He passes them—captured by the song—missing the hand that inches out the sand and reaches for his ankle.

ASHLEY HAWK is a Creative Writing student in Cardiff, Wales, but started writing stories much younger at seven years old. Their stories often include LGBT+ characters and cover a whole range of genres. Whatever suits on the day. They are currently working on writing their first novel, a science-fiction YA Romance.

75

Filtered Through
by Nikki R. Leigh

Ghosts, translucent, filtering light as if soapy bubbles in sun, dance with new life like jellyfish in the ocean. Fishermen. Old sea captains. Divers from expeditions gone wrong.

They don't get a chance to walk the earth, tied to a home or a graveyard. They are tied to the sea; the ever-expansive, deep blue. They swim, no need to hold breaths that have ceased long ago.

They tell their stories to the oxygen trapped in the salty water, scream it into vastness that never reaches ears.

Squinting, I see them, desperately trying to stay remembered after the silence of death.

NIKKI R. LEIGH is a forever-90s-kid wallowing in all things horror. When not writing horror fiction, she can be found creating custom horror-inspired toys, making comics, and hunting vintage paperbacks. She reads her stories to her partner and her cat, one of whom gets scared very easily.
Instagram - @spinetinglers
Twitter - @fivexxfive
Email – spinetinglersmedia@gmail.com

76

Sunken
by Kyle McHugh

Meghan sat suspended, light refracting around her in the clear blue water. She waved her arms to halt her ascent to the surface.

After a moment of peaceful silence, her feet flattened against the vinyl and propelled her towards the surface.

Thud.

Meghan's head hit a shimmering barrier and caused her to wince. In panicked confusion she searched for a spot to break through, slamming her hands against the barrier.

The water pressed inwards against her and pulled her towards the bottom.

Meghan sunk, her chest heavy. Her lungs began to ache. She looked up at the slowly fading sun.

KYLE MCHUGH is a trans author, artist, and educator. He writes poetry and young adult fiction, and believes fostering student voice can lead to positive change. When Kyle is not writing he can be found painting or drawing. He lives in Albany, New York, with his wife and son. You can find him on Twitter @KyleMcHugh119.

77

RIP
by Laura Keating

Abby spiked the ball too hard. The cheap rubber pinged atop the water and was quickly pulled out on a wave. Bryce was a good swimmer; he chased without a second thought.

"I'll get it!"

He swam a full stroke, going fast. He looked around.

The shore was far. Abby was small, shouting. Bryce laughed but couldn't touch bottom. He headed back.

And back.

And back.

Abby was smaller.

And back.

Harder.

The rip was strong.

The ball, a red dot. Gone.

Breath of salt spray.

Panicked hands against an ocean.

Arms heavy.

Abby was small.

Please, God.

Smaller.

Gone.

LAURA KEATING is a writer of thrillers, horror, and speculative fiction. Her work has been published in several anthologies, *including* Worst Laid Plans *from Grindhouse Press, and* Beneath, Cosmos, *and* Rock Band *collections from Ghost Orchid Press. You can follow Laura on Twitter at @LoreKeating, and find more of her work on her website, www.lorekeating.com*

78

Sinking in a Still Life
by Kathryn Bea

At the end of the lane was a weathered farmhouse. At the end of the hallway was a slanted room. At the end of the bed was a faded painting. All turbulent blue depths.

The first night I dreamt of crashing waves and salty air. Light and peaceful.

The second night I dreamt of pointy fins and writhing tentacles. Sharp and stinging.

The third night I dreamt of a dark and boundless abyss. Silent and oppressive.

The fourth night I did not dream. Nor did I wake.

My ears rang, my lungs burned. A torment as infinite as the sea.

KATHRYN BEA is an aspiring writer, avid reader, world traveler, and lover of all things horror and speculative fiction. When she isn't scribbling out stories, she can be found earning money for her next international trip by tormenting patrons in a fantastic escape room in Pittsburgh, Pennsylvania.

79

The Lorelai
by Clarabelle Miray Fields

Twenty years later, it isn't dead, only sleeping, in the river she swam in as a child. It likes the deep, the dark and hidden: backwater edges, waterlogged shadows, places where sunlight and fishermen won't go. But children are different. They will go anywhere, tempted by siren song. A song she knows well from nightmares. A song she can't forget.

Circling closer, she can smell it now. Nauseating, reeking of blood and rotting leaves. She brought a gun, but it's already too late. She only catches a glimpse as she goes under: a child smiling at her, full of teeth.

CLARABELLE MIRAY FIELDS is a writer, web developer, and editor from Boulder, Colorado. She has been published over 100 times, most recently in Corvid Queen, *the* 2021 Rhysling Anthology, *and elsewhere. Find out more at www.clarabellefields.com.*

80

Unlucky Dip
by Emma K. Leadley

The heat reached record temperatures and all we wanted to do was go swimming to cool down. The public pool was closed and the only other one belonged to the dilapidated house at the top of the street. We'd been warned not to trespass, but we were desperate and broke in.

The pool was clear and inviting. We started diving for pennies, progressively working deeper. Jonny dived to find the next coin. He never resurfaced so we jumped in to find him. There was no body. We scrambled out, panicking, but muscular tentacles reached out, pulling us back and under.

EMMA K. LEADLEY (she/they) is a UK-based writer with over 30 indie-published pieces of speculative flash fiction and short stories. She was a Grindstone Literary 2019 Microfiction Winner and Publishers Weekly described one of her stories as 'standout'. She lives in Nottingham, with her husband and a rescue greyhound.

DECOMPRESSION

81

Winter Dreaming
by Georgia Cook

It was cold beneath the ice; cold as cold and dark as sin. The current filled her lungs, tugged her hair, lifted her bones to dance like stringless marionettes between the shafts of sunlight. No sound down here, no summer breeze; the fish lay sleeping leagues below, the reeds had died in the onset frost.

Only Winter, all of Winter, stretched out in velvety black. Patiently waiting.

Soon the ice would crack; soon the world above would shine bright and clear. Soon her hands would reach out, long and white and needle-sharp, and break the surface.

And Winter would rise.

GEORGIA COOK is an illustrator and writer from London. She is the winner of the LISP 2020 Flash Fiction Prize, and has been shortlisted for the Bridport Prize, Staunch Book Prize and Reflex Fiction Award. She can be found on twitter @georgiacooked and her website at https://www.georgiacookwriter.com/.

82

Hand Sown
by Nikki R. Leigh

Seeds are sown beneath the surface, into the blue, the darker blue, the near black. Natural hands did not sow these seeds, but from them, hands will grow.

These tendril-like finders will wrap, then grip and pull and hide those forbidden from being near, which is everyone and everything that are not those hands or their sowers.

At the bottom—the very bottom—they will take you even deeper, under the sand so dark and heavy, unforgiving, to the below, and you will be planted.

They are the hands, you are the seed, and from you, they will grow again.

NIKKI R. LEIGH is a forever-90s-kid wallowing in all things horror. When not writing horror fiction, she can be found creating custom horror-inspired toys, making comics, and hunting vintage paperbacks. She reads her stories to her partner and her cat, one of which gets scared very easily. You can find her on Instagram @spinetinglers or on Twitter @fivexxfive.

83

A Watery Grave
by Blen Mesfin

The sailors all believed having a woman on board was bad luck, and the storm only confirmed their suspicions. It got worse by the minute, threatening to flip the boat over.

It didn't occur to me that they would throw me overboard, not until it was too late. Two of them had already managed to get their grip on me. The boat swayed dangerously as I struggled to get free. Three of them held me down while one tied the ropes around me.

There was a split-second moment when I took my last gasping breath, before getting plunged underwater.

BLEN MESFIN is an Ethiopian writer whose works have appeared in several anthologies. When she's not writing, you will find her nose stuck to the closest book. Writing is a way for her to express herself through characters she will, unfortunately, never meet.

84

Drowning in Sand
by Fusako Ohki

Translated by Toshiya Kamei

Grains of sand dance as heat rises from the earth. You sway on a droopy-eyed camel's back as you tread across an empty expanse of desert. Sweat evaporates off your skin. Your consciousness blurs, and your breathing becomes scratchy. In the distance, a bubbling spring chortles its melody at the foot of a sprawling dune.

"Water!" You kick the camel into a lope.

The spring gushes out of the ground. The water travels down your throat and quenches your thirst. Yet your quivering stomach craves more.

The following day, a search party finds you dead, your mouth stuffed with sand.

FUSAKO OHKI is a Japanese writer from Tokyo. She obtained her master's degree in Japanese literature from Hosei University. Her debut collection of short stories is forthcoming in 2021. Translated by Toshiya Kamei, Fusako's fiction has appeared in New World Writing.

85

Confessional
by Mackenzie Hurlbert

He writes his secret in red Sharpie and sneaks it into a nipper bottle. These days, he yearns for relief—to hear the sirens grow louder, knowing this time they won't fly past. He scribbles his name, deed, apology... He tightens the cap and throws it in the sea.

But plastic cracks easier than bone. Water slips in, drowns the paper, snuffs out secrets. It sinks past the shadows of whales, past the stinging tendrils of jellyfish, to the depths where creatures lurk, eyeless and toothy. Where darkness presses heavily from all directions, like regrets in the dead of night.

MACKENZIE HURLBERT is a Connecticut-based writer with previous publications in Written Tales: Horror, Flash Fiction Magazine, *Five:2:One's* The Sideshow, *and* The Caravel Journal. *She also received honorable mention in Writer's Digest Popular Fiction Awards for her story "Milk Teeth". She studied at Southern Connecticut State University in New Haven, CT.*

WEBSITE: https://mackenziehurlbert.wixsite.com/writer

86

Murk
by S. J. Wilkes

I hate swimming in lakes. Any natural body of water has awful potential. It's the murk, the weeds and fish that graze my heels. Like the hands of drowned people trying to pull me under.

This time when they grab for me, I grab them back. Then down to the bottle green murk, the claylike soil. The sun only visible through muck and waving fronds. I am torn. My chest is a home for crayfish. Leeches roll under my broken skin.

And now I reach.

I am the fronds around your heels and I am going to pull you down.

S. J. WILKES is an author living in Ontario. She fears deep waters and what lives out of sight underneath, because there can't be anything good there. A lover of insects, S. J. Wilkes loves discovering really good bugs. Twitter: @susanjwilkes.

87

Waiting
by Laura Shenton

The man walks calmly along the pier. He likes to be alone at night. Under the stars and above the waves, the promenade is his safe space. The silence allows for reflection. The lack of hustle and bustle from other people is just what he needs to process the thoughts in his whirling mind.

Little does he know that just mere metres beneath the waves, is a siren who loves to sing. There she waits, biding her time in preparation for when finally, she can lull him with her sweet melodies. She wants to take him away from his pain.

The format of the Hundred Word Horror anthology speaks to LAURA SHENTON in a big way as someone who is a huge fan of Edgar Allan Poe. She will be self publishing some gothic horror novellas soon and is also a traditionally published author of several music non-fiction books.
https://www.amazon.co.uk/s?k=Laura+Shenton

88

Baby Blue
by Carla Eliot

My hair feels soft and exquisitely ethereal as I glide my fingers through the long strands. Tilting my head further back into the water, the thick sound of nothing fills my ears. I stare up, towards the amber ball of light in the cloudless, baby-blue sky.

Baby blue.

Baby.

The word floats around my head as I allow the sun's heat to dry my tears.

Then I feel his hand. My son's small hand, pressing against my back.

His words penetrate the nothingness.

"It's okay, Mum."

I smile, salt from my tears tickling my withered lips.

"I'll always be here."

CARLA ELIOT is a UK writer living in Cheshire with her young son and little dog. She enjoys writing moody fictional stories, often encompassing an underlying message and frequently diving into the paranormal. Carla has stories featured in three of the Blood Rites Horror anthologies and several of her other short stories have been accepted by separate publishers. When Carla isn't writing, she's usually reading, enjoying nature, or watching films. You can find her at carlaeliot.com or on Instagram / Twitter @writecarla.

89

Not The Deep Blue Sea
by Renata Pavrey

Darker than the

darkest black

Limitless like the

expansive sky

but confining like a cage

Pulled in all directions

and compressed within

You can implode

or explode

No one to hear a sound

Witnesses choose to remain silent

Your breath stolen

in more than one way

The calmness of the thermocline

Keeps you anything but calm

The seabed is

not a place for repose

Deeper than the

highest mountains

Creatures in the

darkness, lie in wait

Vampire squid

Spiky sea urchins

When blood turns

from red to green

and black

Whoever called it

the deep blue sea

was clearly mistaken

RENATA PAVREY is a nutritionist by profession, specializing in clinical and sports nutrition. She is a Pilates teacher, a trained Odissi dancer, a marathon runner, and bibliophile. Her writings cover a broad spectrum of subjects including dance, literature, running and other sports, health and fitness, nature and wildlife, languages, movies, and music. You can find her @tomes_and_tales and @pilates_positivity_with_ren on Instagram, at https://medium.com/@reneemarianne7 on Medium, and on her blog www.tomesandtales365.wordpress.com.

90

Memories
by April Yates

I once heard it said that water has a memory.

A rather romantic notion, until I learned it relates to soluble compounds.

But what if it were true?

That by sheer willpower I could transfer the essence of me into the cold liquid enveloping me.

That someone could experience my memories when they drank or bathed in this same water.

A version of me travelling through pipes ready to deliver my last testimonial.

They'll see my killer's face peering down at me before closing the lid of the rooftop water-tank, encasing me in darkness.

Maybe, just maybe, I'll have justice.

APRIL YATES lives in Derbyshire with her wife and two fluffy demons masquerading as dogs. She should be working on her novella about the horrors of golden age Hollywood, but is easily distracted by the squirrels in her garden. Find her on Twitter @April_Yates_ and tell her to get back to work, or aprilyates.com.

91

Day Terrors
by L.W. Blackwood

The water seeps down the walls. From my bed, I watch as a tentacle suctions to the thin glass of the window, which is already cracking. In a few minutes, I will drown. It's the same dream I've had all week, except this time, gills have sprouted on my neck. I touch them with tentative fingers, already suffocating.

I wake from the dream, gasping. I can't catch my breath. Grazing my fingers over my skin, I feel the deep grooves of gills in my throat. I stumble to the window and throw it open, but nothing but air rushes in.

L. W. BLACKWOOD is a speculative fiction writer who loves all things horror.

92

Cooked in Broth From the Waist Down
by Alex Shenstone

It looks like knitting.

A blanket on the surface, floating.

When her curiosity catches, it doesn't let up.

Like trawling men, ready to sup.

Lovely hair. Lovely skin.

Lovely scales. Lovely fin.

She's ripest down from the waist.

Cut the shimmering border. Never waste.

She was carved on mass.

Now, she is Lady Carcass.

Torso. Head. Red hair.

Red everywhere.

Droplets off their skin did drip,

When hauling her off their stained ship.

Sinking,

Unblinking.

Prepared fresh.

Still imprinted by knitted mesh.

Ceviche. Sliced.

Cullen Skink. Simmered and diced.

Maiden torsos are out of view.

So, more broth for you?

ALEX SHENSTONE is a transgender UK university student with an inclination towards darker interpretations. He enjoys spending time contemplating darker perspectives, and reimagining classic stories. He has poetry appearing in The Global Youth Review, *and is on Twitter at @AlexakaSatan.*

93

Siphon
by Mike Murphy

Stephanie turned the sink's cold knob. Nothing issued forth, but she suddenly became terribly ill. Her vomit made an impossible, acrobatic loop in the air and went up the faucet. She was puking water and couldn't stop.

In the vanity mirror, she saw herself rapidly becoming gaunt. Moments later, she wheezed and collapsed onto the tiles—now just the skeletal bits of waste that remain when a body is waterless.

Her final vomit drops went up the pipe.

The planet was delighted at its success and looked forward to getting much more of its resources back from the wasteful humans.

MIKE MURPHY has had over 150 audio plays produced in the U.S. and overseas. He's won The Columbine Award and a dozen Moondance International Film Festival awards in their TV pilot, audio play, short screenplay, and short story categories. His prose work has appeared in several magazines and anthologies. Mike is the writer of two short films, DARK CHOCOLATE and HOTLINE.
In 2013, he won the inaugural Marion Thauer Brown Audio Drama Scriptwriting Competition. In 2020, he came in second. For several of the in-between years, he served as a judge. Mike keeps a blog at audioauthor.blogspot.com.

94

Sexual Tension Resolved in a Benthic Zone Embrace
by Clint White

"Assignment of a *lifetime*," the engineer told him upon his arrival. Her eyes deepwater grey, her voice mixing flirtation and consummate professionalism. He'd laughed, looked away. Three weeks alone with her in this seabed laboratory? Should be... intriguing.

The next day, cleaning the lab window exteriors, he noticed her leering at him through the glass. He stared dumbly, heart depressurizing.

Clouds of seabed sediment surrounded him then. The engineer's form dimmed, hands splayed against thick glass. Was she screaming? Laughing?

A shadow overtook him from behind; numerous arms encircled him. He wailed, breathing apparatus disentangling, his face mocking the eager engineer's.

CLINT WHITE is an environmental lawyer living, working, and writing weird fiction (and the occasional indignant letter to the local paper's editor) in Columbus, Ohio. His flash fiction has previously appeared in Alluvian and is forthcoming in Black Hare Press' 666 anthology. You can find him on Twitter here: @clintrwhite.

95

Atargatis
by K.L. Lord

Moonlight glitters off the dark current, a sweet song rises from the depths. The crystalline notes resonate in my soul. She offers only death. Yet, I step across the tidal line in the sand. Water laps against my shins. My thighs. Her voice rings louder, clearer, the deeper I go.

"I can't," I say.

"Be my love, my pretty thing."

"Please." I try to step back.

Scales graze my bare flesh. A sob escapes my trembling lips. Her song lulls me. I open my eyes and see her for the first time. Beautiful and terrifying. My goddess of the deep.

K.L. LORD writes horror and poetry and has published in both fiction and academic markets. She has an MFA in Writing Popular Fiction from Seton Hill University and is pursuing her Ph.D. in English. You can find her (in non-Covid times) lurking in bookstores, libraries, and tattoo shops.

96

Decompression
by Emma E. Murray

It took only a moment. A fraction of a second. The pressure released before a single worry, prayer, even thought could be formed by the divers. No screams of pain as their torsos burst, unraveled like sinew ribbons, hurrying every secret, dark organ out into the open ocean. Forced through the impossibly small crack in the diving bell that beckoned as an exit, an escape from bodily imprisonment.

Blood-tinged water attracted fish to bask and nibble in the debris, once human, now unrecognizable. Red, raw flotsam, diluted then swept away by currents, leaving behind only shells of bone and skin.

EMMA E. MURRAY is a writer whose novels and short stories explore the dark side of humanity. She spends her days taking care of her daughter and her nights writing. You can find her at EmmaEMurray.com and on Twitter @EMurrayAuthor

97

Sorrow
by Cristina dos Santos

She wraps the sea around her shoulders.

The boy stares into her oyster eyes and plays with a strand of her hair;

it's made of kelp but he cannot tell.

She licks her salt-cracked lips, ignoring the desperate warning of the tide.

Wet sand under her rotted fishbone fingers,

she thirsts for the promise his hands make on her coral skin and

reaches for his eager mouth with barracuda teeth.

He moans (cries,) insistent and demanding.

She relents, pouring all of herself

Writhing writhing, he pulls back, choking

but it's too late.

Always too late, the mourning sea whispers.

CRISTINA DOS SANTOS writes Gothic Horror novels for Young Adults. When she's not dreaming up new nightmares to write about, she's exploring the mountains of North Carolina where she lives with her husband and their two awesome kids. You can find her on Instagram at @dossantosbooks.

98

Beyond the Sea
by Jameson Grey

The sailboat's systems had been on the fritz for a while, leaving Charles to navigate old school. Through the telescope, he'd sighted a ship in the distance—an old schooner.

A gust had drawn his attention away, primarily to check the boom. When he looked up, he was alone again.

Wherever the schooner had gone, he was headed too. The sudden wind ensured that. Although the sky remained perfect blue, something was wrong with the horizon. It seemed sharper.

Charles sailed onward. The horizon loomed large beyond the sea. Grimly, he followed the schooner over the edge of the world.

JAMESON GREY is originally from England but now lives with his family in western Canada. He also spent time in Asia as a child, which he understands makes him a fully-fledged third culture kid (TCK). His fiction and poetry have been published by Ghost Orchid Press, Black Hare Press and Hellbound Books. He can be found online (occasionally) at jameson-grey.com and on Twitter @thejamesongrey.

99

Melody and Toxin:
A Memory Deeper Than Blood
by Melissa Rose Rogers

Shanties cease as the storm swirls a lone ship.

Just what we need. Pearl thinks. *No—what we crave.*

Buffeted, the boat's hull groans.

"Now," Voluta shrieks.

Green vapor pours from the sirens' throats. Wind disperses the melody and toxin, stupefying the sailors before the sirens board the ship.

Pearl shivers as she drinks the sailors' blood; consuming their minds is bliss. Trident to jugular, the men had no chance.

The storm fades, so the sirens recline on the unmanned vessel.

"One of my victims made new songs," Voluta says.

Pearl scoffs, "Their shanties were as meaningless as their lives."

MELISSA ROSE ROGERS *writes speculative fiction and recently moved to Denver, CO, with her husband, daughters, and kitties. Her fiction appears in Bear Creek Gazette, Tales from the Moonlit Path, 96th of October, Harvey Duckman Presents, and Bewildering Stories. Her website is https://melissaroserogers.com/. She retweets excessively @MRogersWrites*

100

Homecoming
by Kristin Cleaveland

The dreams were driving me mad. I'd wake up covered in sweat, gasping for breath. Remembering faint glimpses of an ancient city beneath the waves. My legs caught in the sheets, tied together tightly. My lips tasting of salt.

I'd long ago left the place near the sea where I was born. One morning, after another restless night, I got in my car and drove until I heard the crashing of the waves.

At the water's edge, I watched the tide roll in. The sunken city was calling me home. I took a deep breath, and walked into the sea.

KRISTIN CLEAVELAND writes horror and dark fiction. Her work has been published by Ghost Orchid Press, Quill and Crow Publishing House, Black Telephone Magazine, *and more. Find her on Twitter as @KristinCleaves.*

ACKNOWLEDGEMENTS

This is our fourth Hundred Word Horror anthology, and that fact alone is amazing to me. Once more, I must thank all the contributors, and everyone who kindly sent their stories in for consideration. I thoroughly enjoyed reading them all, and I'm only sorry there wasn't space for more. A further thank you to our fantastic supporters: everyone who has ever bought one of our books, joined our Patreon, spread the word on social media or offered encouragement and kind words. Without you, we would simply not be here.

Much love,

Antonia

ALSO AVAILABLE FROM GHOST ORCHID PRESS

Check out the other books in our Hundred Word Horror series.

https://ghostorchidpress.com